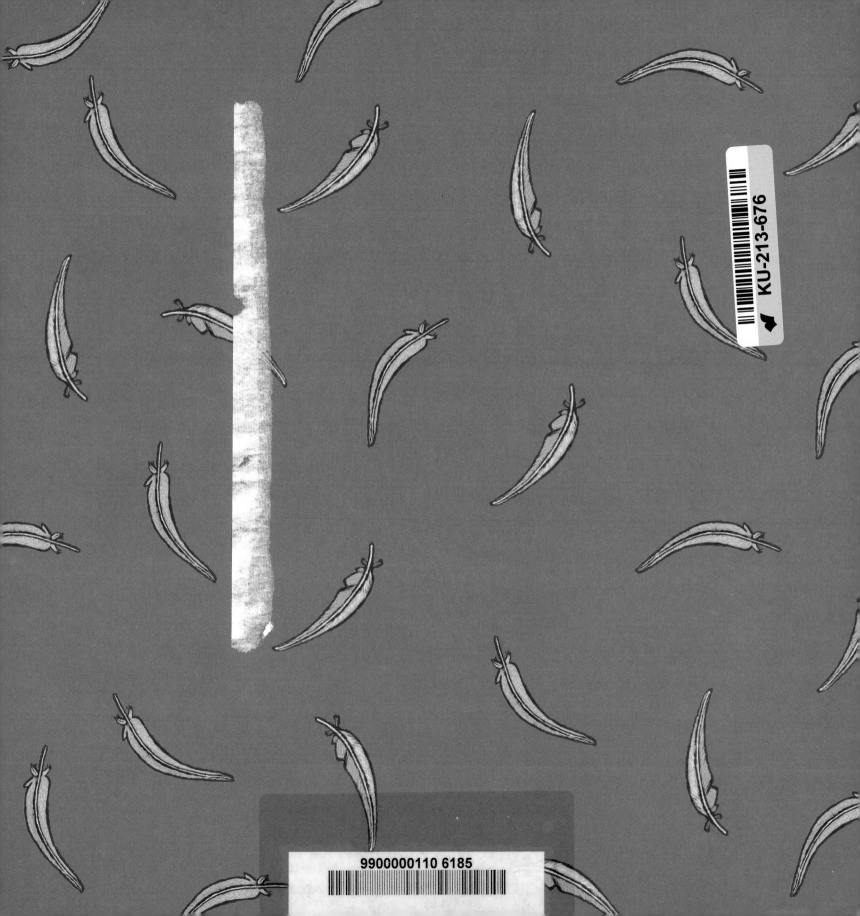

KU-213-676

9900000110 6185

PETERBOROUGH LIBRARIES	
6185	
Bertrams	30.03.08
JF/PIC	£10.99

COCK-A-DOODLE-DOO!

Written by Cecily Matthews
Illustrated by Lorette Broekstra

LITTLE  HARE
www.littleharebooks.com

Basil was **big** and **bossy**.

Leonard was peaky and puny.

Basil's job was to
wake the farm.

Leonard thought he was too small to try.

Every morning Basil
strutted and shoved.

'COCK-A-DOODLE-DOO!'

His noisy crowing woke the farmer.
The farmer got up.
And then the farmer milked
the cows and fed the hens.

But one day ...

'Crkkk.
Crkkk.'

Basil couldn't wake the farmer.
The farmer didn't milk the cows.
And he didn't feed the hens.

The hens gathered around Leonard.
'You'll have to wake the farmer, sonny.'

'But I can't,'
Leonard whispered.
'I'm not big like Basil.
I'm not burly like Basil.'

Leonard crept away to hide.

His legs went
wibble-wobble ...

He squeezed
his eyes shut.

... wibble-wobble.

The hens found him.
They clucked and fussed.

'Leonard, you have to
wake the farm,' they said.
'We want our breakfast.'
'But I can't,' Leonard whispered.

Leonard hung his head.
The hens were right.

He ran away.
He ran and ran until he
found himself in the dairy.

The cows looked down at him.
'You have to wake the farmer,'
they said. 'We want to be milked.'

'But I can't,' Leonard whispered.

'He's just a shrimp,' snorted one cow.
'No one would hear him.'
'A pipsqueak,' said another.
Leonard's head hung lower. The cows were right.

The cows wished the farmer
would wake up. They pushed
against each other and
stamped their feet.

'Please don't stamp on me!' Leonard cried.

The cows didn't hear him.

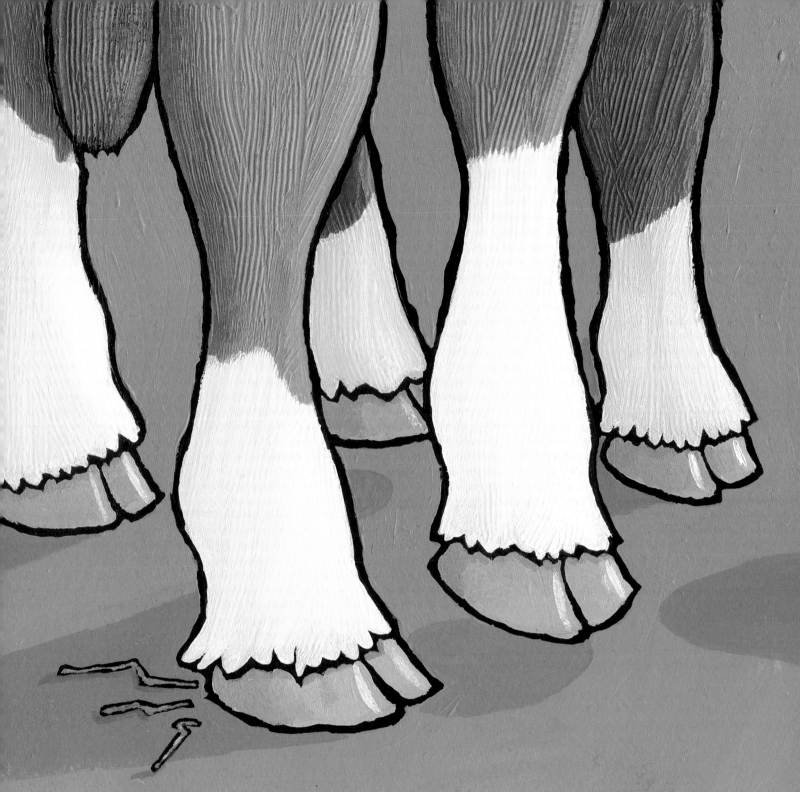

He said it again, louder. And then again.

And suddenly ...

The cows stopped stamping.
The hens stopped clucking.
The farmer jumped out of bed.

And from then on, Leonard always woke the farm.

COCK-A-DOO

For Georgina and Jemma, my newest little chicks — CM
For Jude — LB

Little Hare Books
8/21 Mary Street, Surry Hills
NSW 2010 AUSTRALIA

www.littleharebooks.com

Copyright © text Cecily Matthews 2008
Copyright © illustrations Lorette Broekstra 2008

First published in 2008

All rights reserved. No part of this publication may be reproduced,
stored in a retrieval system or transmitted in any form or by any
means, electronic, mechanical, photocopying, recording or
otherwise, without the prior written permission of the publisher.

National Library of Australia
Cataloguing-in-Publication entry

Matthews, Cecily, 1945- .
Cock-a-doodle-doo.

For children.
ISBN 978 1 921272 06 6 (hbk).

1. Self-esteem - Juvenile fiction. 2. Roosters - Juvenile
fiction. I. Broekstra, Lorette. II. Title.

A823.3

Designed by Vida Kelly
Printed in China through Phoenix Offset

5 4 3 2 1